The Mouse's Discovery: Chancel Plays for Young and Old

Edited by John McTavish

I0741579

Baker's Plays
7611 Sunset Blvd.
Los Angeles, CA 90042
BAKERSPLAYS.COM

The Publisher acknowledges that *Tomorrow We Go To Bethlehem* and *A Word With You* were originally published by Abingdon Press, and *The Good Samaritan* by Richard Coleman is adapted from a piece published by CCS Publishing Company under the title *Gospel Telling*.

THE MOUSE'S DISCOVERY: CHANCEL PLAYS FOR YOUNG AND OLD
ISBN 978-0-87440-233-9
2018-B

CONTENTS

PREFACE

There is emotional power and theological stimulation in these sim-ple-to-produce plays. There's also mischief and mirth and maximum opportunity for participation.

Tomorrow We Go to Bethlehem, A Word with You and *The Third Wish* are all Christmas plays designed for a mix of teenage and adult actors. *The Mouse's Discovery* is a Christmas pageant involving the entire church school. *The Good Samaritan* is a pantomime that the whole congregation can perform with the worship leader. And *The Face of Jesus* is a two-hander for adult actors.

So that's our pitch. Throw away those bulky bathrobes! Invite everyone to participate! Embrace the element of play in these thought-provoking chancel dramas!

You won't be disappointed.

–John McTavish

TOMORROW WE GO TO BETHLEHEM

by Patricia Wells

CHARACTERS

TOUR GUIDE – a retired clergyman
FIRST WOMAN – tourist
SECOND WOMAN – tourist
MIDDLE-AGED HUSBAND AND WIFE – tourists
FATHER – tourist
MIKE – twelve year-old son
JOSEPH
MARY

(A group of people moves up the middle aisle of the church looking around curiously. The people are dressed as tourists and have the usual tourist paraphernalia – cameras, sunglasses, tote bags.)

TOUR GUIDE. And now, my good people, with this historic city of Jericho we conclude another day in our tour of the Holy Land. Are there any further questions before we move back to the bus?

FIRST WOMAN. *(in a stage whisper to her friend)* It may be the oldest inhabited city in the world, but I can't imagine why anyone would want to live here. My lungs are clogged with dust.

SECOND WOMAN. *(nodding in agreement)* Right now I'd trade my soul for a nice air-conditioned hotel room.

FIRST WOMAN. I just hope there's more hot water than we had last night!

SECOND WOMAN. I know. I've certainly been on better organized tours. You'd think that if that hotel knew we were coming, they'd at least have gotten in some decent diet drinks.

GUIDE. Right, ladies and gentlemen. I know you want to get back for a nice long soak in the tub and a little nap before dinner, so I won't keep you any longer. Tomorrow is a very special day. Tomorrow we go to Bethlehem. The buses will be at the door by eight o'clock, so get to bed early tonight. I'll see you bright and chipper at breakfast, no later than seven. Thank you.

HUSBAND. O Lord, not another bus tour. That bus is like a blast furnace!

WIFE. I just hope he gets us back in time for some shopping tomorrow afternoon.

(They watch **MIKE***, the only child on the tour, kick a can around.)*

People shouldn't bring kids on these tours. They have no appreciation of what's going on.

(The group goes off to the side, or possibly sits in the front pews. A girl in a plain brown dress or robe comes in and sits on a bench on one side of the chancel, opposite to where the tourists exited. After a few seconds a young man comes in and sits beside her.)

JOSEPH. I'm sorry, Mary. I've tried everything I know. We'll have to go to Bethlehem tomorrow.

MARY. I can't, Joseph. You'll just have to leave me here. I'm seven months pregnant. I can't travel eighty miles over rough roads. I can't risk losing this baby. It's my first baby, and it's – very special.

JOSEPH. *(bitterly)* Do you think that means anything to the Romans? When I asked if I could register you, they just laughed. We're a joke to them. A bad, money-making joke. We're taxes. Roman justice doesn't apply to us, Mary. Life on this earth was made for the rich. That's the way it's always been and that's the way it's always going to be.

*(***MARY*** *bows her head and then shakes it slowly and looks up at him.)*

MARY. I don't think so Joseph. I mean, I know that's how it looks, and maybe that's how it's always been. But I believe our prophets. God really does see our troubles and one day – soon – he'll come to defend us, One day he will put down the mighty from their seats and lift up the poor. I know that sounds *unlikely*, but I believe it. And for now – well, I guess we'll just have to manage.

*(***JOSEPH*** *puts his arm around her at they walk to the side. The tourists re-enter.)*

GUIDE. This chapel represents the official site where the shepherds saw the angels. There's a lovely view from here over Bethlehem. And a short way down the road is the kind of shelter that Mary and Joseph probably stayed in. Now, this is something you'll want to tell your friends back home. Mary and Joseph probably didn't stay in what we consider a stable. It's likely they stayed in one of these small animal shelters, really just a small cave or rocky overhang where they herded the animals in bad weather.

MIKE. *(speaking to his father at the back of the crowd)* Dad, how many more churches do we have to look at? They're so boring!

FATHER. Don't you realize, Mike, this is the most important town in the world?

MIKE. You really think so? More important than L.A. or The Big Apple?

FATHER. Yes, it is.

MIKE. Well, I guess…I just don't see the point of walking around some dirty old primitive town. I've got a new video game I want to play back at the hotel. How long is this going to take?

FATHER. *(exasperated)* I don't know!

*(**MIKE** starts to kick the can back and forth.)*

FATHER. Look, Mike. Stop kicking that can. We brought you on this trip so you'd have some appreciation of – Christianity. This is where our faith started. That should be important to you. It's important to me.

*(**MIKE** looks at him seriously, but then after a few seconds goes back to kicking the can.)*

FATHER. *(voice slightly raised)* Just get rid of that can!

GUIDE. *(Speaking more animatedly, but the tour group, with the exception of* **MIKE***, begins to lose interest, and starts to look around. As the guide talks on,* **MIKE** *moves closer in to the front.)* Mary was quite young, you know, probably only about fourteen, just a kid really. Well, you can imagine the cave with the stench from the animals, the cold, the loneliness, the pain…(sees his audience's attention is wandering) Yes, well it is difficult…I know most of you are eager to get back to the hotel and have dinner, so we won't take the time to enter it today. But we can stop at the Blessed Virgin Gift Shop on the way out. You can pick up postcards if you like. They've also got nativity creches, beautiful hand made...Right. Let's move along then...

FIRST WOMAN. I don't know why he wants to spoil the Christmas story for us. I think it's lovely the way it is in the Bible.

*(They walk off, but **MIKE** remains. **MARY** and **JOSEPH** re-enter, walking slowly. **MIKE** stands to one side listening as they talk.)*

MARY. I can't go any farther, Joseph. I really don't feel well. Anyway, we've tried all the inns in town. There's no place else to go.

(They sit down close together on a bench looking dejected. A moment or so passes.)

JOSEPH. That last place had an animal shelter out back. I'll go ask about it. It would be better than nothing.

*(He goes off briefly while **MARY** remains huddled on the bench.)*

JOSEPH. *(returning)* It's all right. Let's go. You can have my tunic for an extra blanket. It's going to be cold tonight.

MARY. I can't take it. You'll freeze!

JOSEPH. Come on, and don't argue. It's my tunic!

*(**MARY** laughs goodnaturedly, but as **JOSEPH** helps her to her feet, she staggers.)*

MARY. Joseph, I'm so *scared*.

*(As they go slowly off, **MIKE** walks up into the pulpit and reads carefully and clearly Luke 2: 1- 19: "In those days a decree went out from Caesar Augustus..." ending with, "But Mary kept all these things, pondering them in her heart.")*

A WORD WITH YOU

by Marney Heatley and Brian Martin

CHARACTERS

MR. MATTHEWS – manager of shepherds
SIMON, **MARTHA**, **RACHEL**, **BEN** – shepherds
BECKY – young stable helper
BETH – Simon's wife
BABY – Simon and Beth's baby

Scene One

(**MR. MATTHEWS** *is sitting at a desk, working diligently at some papers. Nearby on a bench,* **BEN**, **MARTHA**, *and* **RACHEL** *are talking amongst themselves.* **SIMON** *enters, carrying his lunch bucket, smiling, and walking with a bounce in his step. He approaches* **MR. MATTHEWS**, *who is engrossed in his work.*)

SIMON. *(sheepishly)* Good morning, Mr. Mathews.

MATTHEWS. *(without looking up)* Good morning. *(looks up and sarcastically)* Ah, Simon. Decided to pay us a visit, did you?

SIMON. Yes, well, I'm sorry about missing work yesterday.

MATTHEWS. I hope you have a good excuse. I could use a few chuckles today.

SIMON. Well, you see, sir, it's my wife. She –

MATTHEWS. Never mind. Your absence didn't make much difference anyway. Not with all the commotion that went on over at Hill Twelve last night.

SIMON. Sir?

MATTHEWS. I'm sure you'll hear all about it before long. It's all anyone seems to be able to talk about around here.

(pauses to write something down on a piece of paper, which he then hands to **SIMON**)

You're working Hill Seven this afternoon. And keep an eye out. We've had quite a few strays lately.

SIMON. *(taking the paper)* Thank you, sir.

*(***SIMON** *leaves* **MR. MATTHEWS** *at his desk and approaches the others. They are excitedly discussing something and don't notice* **SIMON***'s approach.*)

SIMON. Hi, guys. What's all the fuss about?

(The others jump up and start talking at once.)

SIMON. Hold on a minute. One at a time.

MARTHA. You missed the most amazing thing last night, Simon.

SIMON. What?

RACHEL. It was like nothing I've ever seen before in my life.

MARTHA. It was real cold last night, bone-chilling cold. Rachel and I were watching over Mr. Matthews' favourites, when all of a sudden this rush of warm air came out of nowhere, and there was a soft glow, sort of like moonlight, only bright enough to read by.

BEN. This light, it covered four or five hills at least. I saw it too, and I was way over on Sixteen.

RACHEL. Then there was this flash, and a weird sort of humming noise.

BEN. By now, the sheep were going nuts, bleating and running around like crazy.

RACHEL. I was scared to death.

BEN. I've seen a lot of weird things in my day, but never anything like this.

MARTHA. And then *he* appeared.

SIMON. Who appeared?

MARTHA. I don't know. I guess he was an angel. All I know is that he was a messenger from God.

SIMON. *(entranced)* What was the message?

RACHEL. The Savior is born. Here, in our town.

BEN. Then there were millions of these angels all singing.

RACHEL. And the weird thing was, I knew they were singing "Glory to God," even though they weren't using words. It was like I heard it with my heart and not my ears.

BEN. It was a show like no other. The kind of thing theatre producers dream about. A production number with a cast of thousands, and then they were gone *(snaps his fingers)* – just like that.

MARTHA. It was dazzling.

RACHEL. I would have thought I'd dreamed it all except for this lingering sweet smell in the air. I couldn't help feeling that I'd just witnessed the most important thing in the world.

MARTHA. Just think – the Savior! In our time and our town. Oh Simon, God has truly blessed us!

SIMON. Someone who didn't know you three as well as I do might be excused for thinking you were in the sauce last night. But that's okay. It was pretty cold.

RACHEL. Don't be funny, Simon. We're serious. This could be the thing we've been waiting for all our lives.

SIMON. Did you go into town then? Did you go and see this great marvel?

MARTHA. We tried to. We asked Mr. Matthews for permission to go. But he refused.

SIMON. That's Matthews all right.

BEN. He said he'd heard excuses before, but this really took the cake.

RACHEL. He told us we'd all be fired if we left the sheep.

SIMON. If what you say was as important as you insist, why didn't you go anyway?

MARTHA. Come on Simon, you know how times are. If we lose our jobs our families will starve.

RACHEL. I'd think you'd be especially concerned about that, Simon. What with Beth expecting and all.

SIMON. Oh, I meant to tell you. Beth had the baby – a girl! That's why I was away yesterday.

MARTHA. Oh Simon, that's marvellous.

BEN. Congratulations, 'Dad.'

RACHEL. I guess you experienced your own little miracle last night.

SIMON. A baby is a pretty special thing.

RACHEL. Yeah.

MARTHA. We're really happy for you, Simon, but what are we going to do about this other baby?

SIMON. I think we should go into town. I don't think Mr. Matthews would fire us. I know he comes across as a tyrant. But he's really a nice guy.

MARTHA. Maybe, but what happens if he decides to follow through on his threat?

SIMON. Let's at least talk to him.

BEN. Well, okay. I guess it's at least worth a try. Let's go.

(*They approach* MR. MATTHEWS *at his desk.*)

MARTHA. Excuse me, sir.

MATTHEWS. What is it? Why aren't you out in the fields yet?

MARTHA. We've been talking about what happened last night. We feel that it's important to go into town and check it out.

MATTHEWS. Look, I've got a business to run here. I can't afford to have half a shift running off, chasing the results of last night's overindulgences.

SIMON. If I may, sir, I've only heard about this second-hand, but there's something about it that I can't shake loose.

RACHEL. You know us, Mr. Matthews. We wouldn't ask to go if it wasn't important.

MARTHA. We won't be long.

MATTHEWS. Who's going to mind the sheep?

BEN. Actually, sir, we've thought of that. John in the far field owes me a favour. I'm sure he'll keep a watch on our flocks.

MARTHA. We'd like your permission, but we're going even if you don't give it.

MATTHEWS. (*resignedly*) Very well, but please hurry back.

MARTHA. Thank you, sir.

(*They all turn to go.*)

RACHEL. (*turning back*) Why don't you come with us?

MATTHEWS. (*considering and then rejecting the offer*) No, no, there's too much to do here. I really can't.

RACHEL. Come on, sir. The place will survive without you for a few hours.

MATTHEWS. (*softening*) Well... I guess... (*looking at the papers on his desk*) No, I've got all these census forms to finish up. Got to keep the government happy, you know. No, you four go – with my good wishes.

RACHEL. Thank you, sir.

(SHEPHERDS *exit.*)

Scene Two

*(**SHEPHERDS** approach the stable, indicated by a bale or two of straw.)*

BEN. *(pointing up)* Look, there's the star we're supposed to follow.

SIMON. It's coming to rest over the Ritz Hotel.

MARTHA. The Ritz! Of course. We should have guessed that ourselves.

RACHEL. Do they have mangers at the Ritz?

SIMON. Mangers?

RACHEL. I thought the angels said something about "lying in a manger."

MARTHA. With all that ruckus, it was hard to tell what they were saying. They probably said – um – "lying with an angel."

BEN. Look, the star is moving again.

(They all look up.)

MARTHA. Why is it moving? This is the best hotel in town.

SIMON. I don't know. It's disappeared behind that turret.

BEN. Let's go.

RACHEL. Wait.

BEN. What now?

RACHEL. I'm scared. Think of the show those angels put on. And that was just the introduction. Will common shepherds like us be able to look on the face of the Savior? Or will it be just too much for us?

MARTHA. That's a chance we have to take, Rachel. If God has chosen to bless us in this way, how can we refuse him?

SIMON. What better chance have we to worship God than this?

BEN. Let's get going before the star gets too far ahead of us.

*(The others start to leave but **RACHEL** appears to be holding back.)*

MARTHA. Stay or come, Rachel. It's your choice. But don't come whining to us if you miss the opportunity of a lifetime.

RACHEL. I'll come.

(**BEN** and **SIMON** *have moved a little closer to the stable.* **RACHEL** and **MARTHA** *now catch up to them.*)

SIMON. There's the star.

RACHEL. How come it stopped over that barn?

BEN. Give it a minute. It'll move again.

SIMON. I don't think so.

MARTHA. This is ridiculous.

RACHEL. You think we misheard about the star, too?

BEN. We must have. Let's go back and check the hotel.

SIMON. I'm going to see what's in the barn.

MARTHA. Come on, Simon. It'll be a waste of time.

BEN. I don't want to hobnob with sheep any more than I have to.

(*At this point* **BECKY** *comes running in, her arms laden with swaddling clothes. She brushes past the shepherds and calls into the stable.*)

BECKY. I brought the swaddling clothes, and the kitchen boy at the hotel promised to lend me his blanket.

RACHEL. Swaddling clothes? The angels said something about swaddling clothes!

BECKY. I'll be right back.

(*She leaves, brushing by the shepherds once more.*)

BEN. I don't like this.

SIMON. What do you think it means?

MARTHA. I don't know. (*grasping at straws – figuratively, that is*) Maybe it was all a practical joke.

RACHEL. But all those lights and the music. How do you explain that?

BEN. (*tentatively*) They do it with mirrors?

SIMON. Do you really believe that?

BEN. *(confused)* I don't know what I believe.

MARTHA. Oh, Simon, I know it wasn't a joke. It was real and it was important, but now everything seems so confusing. I don't know what to think anymore.

SIMON. What if you heard right about the manger and the swaddling clothes? What if the Son of God is really in that stable?

MARTHA. We're poor people, Simon. We have to earn our living working with animals. We don't have any choice. But do you think Almighty God, who can do whatever he wants, is going to choose to come into the world in a cold, smelly stable?

BEN. Of course not. I mean, he wouldn't let his people down like that. We asked for a king.

SIMON. Maybe we got a king. Let's look closer.

MARTHA. Come on, guys, we're obviously in the wrong place. Let's go back and ask at the hotel.

(MARTHA and BEN turn to go. BECKY returns with a larger blanket rumpled into a ball.)

BECKY. Have you come to worship the baby too?

RACHEL. We're looking for the King of the Jews.

BEN. *(to MARTHA)* If he's not at the 'Ritz, we could check out the Park Plaza.

MARTHA. Are you coming Simon? Rachel?

SIMON. I'll be along in a minute.

(MARTHA and BEN start to go. RACHEL looks hesitatingly at SIMON and then at the other two.)

RACHEL. *(to MARTHA and BEN)* Wait for me!

(RACHEL leaves with MARTHA and BEN. SIMON stands in front of the stable with BECKY. During the previous exchange, BECKY has been fussing with the blanket, but it is too big for her to handle.)

BECKY. *(to SIMON)* Do you think you could help me with this? It's a bit too big for me.

SIMON. Sure.

(He moves forward and helps her fold it.)

BECKY. Thanks.

SIMON. Do you believe that this baby is the Son of God?

BECKY. Uh huh.

SIMON. How do you know?

BECKY. I just know.

SIMON. Nobody told you?

BECKY. No, I guess not.

(They finish folding the blanket.)

SIMON. There. All done.

BECKY. You could help me carry the water bucket if you wanted to. It's kinda heavy when it's full.

SIMON. How come you're doing all this? Do you know these people?

BECKY. Sure. They're Mary and Joseph and the baby Jesus. I met them this morning.

SIMON. *(picking up the bucket and carrying it a short distance)* Are you always this helpful to people you hardly know?

BECKY. I have to do something. I'm poor, so I don't have anything else to give the baby as a present.

SIMON. I don't have anything to give either.

BECKY. That's okay. You helped. *(putting the swaddling clothes in the bucket)* There. Those should soak for a while. Well, I'd better get going. If I'm away too long, my mom gets worried. Bye.

SIMON. Bye. *(He looks into the stable thoughtfully, then gradually turns and walks away.)*

Scene Three

(BETH is seated in a rocking chair, with her baby cradled in her arms. She is looking anxious. She gets up, goes to the window and looks out, and then sits down again. Finally SIMON comes in.)

BETH. Simon! Where have you been? I've been worried sick.

(SIMON kisses BETH and the baby.)

SIMON. How's the little one?

BETH. Fine, but what about you? Ruth next door said she saw you downtown. Why weren't you at work?

SIMON. Did you hear about the commotion in the fields last night?

BETH. It's all over town. They say there were angels announcing the birth of the Savior.

SIMON. That's why I was in town. I went to see him. A baby called Jesus.

BETH. What did he look like? I imagine him looking like those little cherubs painted on the walls in the town hall.

SIMON. Actually, he looks a lot like our baby – like any baby.

BETH. Did he have a halo?

SIMON. No. And he was born in a stable.

BETH. *(taking it in)* That wasn't what I was expecting.

SIMON. That wasn't what any of us were expecting. Martha, Ben, and Rachel all left. They thought they were in the wrong place.

BETH. Why did you stay?

SIMON. I don't know – curiosity maybe. But I met a little girl there. She was helping out, fetching and carrying, worshipping in her own way. Seeing her faith made me realize how little I had.

BETH. I guess children have a lot to teach us. They don't let things get in the way of their love.

SIMON. It was hard to understand what I saw in that stable. Joseph and Mary – who's ever heard of them? Poor nobodies holed up in a cold, dirty barn. Then they give birth to this child, and put him in the straw where the cows come to eat. It looked like a scene of lowly human squalor. We see it every day of our lives. It took a child's faith to make me realize that it was more than that – much more. That baby is the Son of God. *(pausing to look at Beth and particularly the baby)* But why? Why did God choose this way to come into the world? It doesn't make sense to me.

*(A moment of silence. **BETH** studies the baby in her arms, and then looks up at **SIMON**.)*

BETH. You know, maybe it does make sense.

*(**SIMON** looks down at her. She gets up and hands him the baby. He rocks it gently, looking warmly at it.)*

BETH. How could God understand us if he were to just sit up in heaven on his throne, like some people say he does?

SIMON. *(catching on)* But if God came to earth as a baby and grew up with us, he would know what it was like.

BETH. Exactly.

SIMON. But why did God come to earth as a poor child? He could reach more people as a great king, couldn't he?

BETH. Maybe. But who touches your life more, a king or a friend?

SIMON. I suppose we're used to tuning out the voices of authority by now, but we can't ignore one of our own.

BETH. They say he was born last night. Just think – he has the same birthday as our little one.

SIMON. *(looking at the baby)* Maybe they'll grow up together. Wouldn't that be exciting?

BETH. *(taking the baby back and speaking to it)* I pray that you get a chance to meet this Jesus, play with him – learn a little of what he knows.

SIMON. God knows we need some guidance. Life under Herod isn't easy for anyone, man or child.

BETH. Well, we can be sure of some help now. God's put in a good word for us.

THE THIRD WISH

A Play for Christmas

by Jim Taylor

PLAYERS

RACHEL – the owner of Rachel's Tavern. *(The Tomb belongs to another Rachel, the wife of Jacob alias Israel, who died several centuries earlier.)*

SARAH – the waitress, Miriam's mother, from Magdala.

MIRIAM – a young girl also from Magdala in Galilee *(could be between 8 and 14; could even be a boy, with some minor adjustment of lines).*

HINDU – one of the three wise ones from the east *(think of Mahatma Gandhi in travel clothes).*

BUDDHIST – one of the three wise ones from the east *(saffron robes and sandals).*

ISLAM – one of the three wise ones from the east. *(Yes, yes,* **ISLAM** *did not come into existence until 600 years after Jesus' birth, but it is a major world religion, and therefore worth including. For costume, think of Mohamed – long beard, turban, flowing robes.)*

(Note: The three wise ones are caricatures, and not intended to represent in any way the true nature of the three religious groups – any more than Herod represents all monarchs.)

GUARD – who bodyguards Herod and also hands out parking tickets.

KING HEROD – a kind of Mafia Godfather to the Jerusalem area.

CLERK – who bows and scrapes and checks the authoritative scriptures.

(Of the above, **SARAH**, *and* **RACHEL** *must be women; the* **GUARD** *and* **KING HEROD** *must be male. The rest of the characters could be either sex, though probably at least* **ISLAM** *of the wise ones should be male.)*

SCENE

Rachel's Tomb and Tavern, about half way between Jerusalem and Bethlehem. There are four tables set out. The setting requires at least two exits, a front door and a kitchen door. Ideally, the front door should contain translucent glass, through which can be seen the shadows of people and animals outside.

(**SARAH** *is busy setting and cleaning tables, while* **RACHEL** *watches.*)

RACHEL. *(seizing the cutlery* **SARAH** *has been setting out) No*, no, no! Side plates over here, glasses there. Remember: you drink from the right, and eat from the left!

SARAH. Yes'm.

RACHEL. My customers expect you to get it right.

SARAH. Yes'm.

RACHEL. And make sure your little girl doesn't get in the way. *(She sweeps majestically out the kitchen door.)*

(**MIRIAM** *enters with a coloring book.*)

MIRIAM. Mom? What color do I do God?

SARAH. Whatever you want, dear.

MIRIAM. No, Mom, what color is God?

SARAH. What are you coloring?

MIRIAM. This book that Aunt Mary gave me, about God creating the earth out of nothing.

SARAH. Oh, that one.

MIRIAM. So what color is God?

SARAH. *(stalling for time)* Well, you know, dear, that our Scriptures tell us that humans were created in God's image, but of course, humans come in lots of different colors. We're sort of light brown, I guess, but there are people way up in the north, in places like Sweden and Canada, who are much lighter skinned. Almost pink, you know. (**MIRIAM** *looks puzzled.*) About the color of a baby piglet. (**MIRIAM** *nods.*) And the people who come from India tend to be more dark brown. But there are other people who live to the south of us, from Ethiopia and Sheba, who are almost black – in the sun they sometimes look bluey-black.

MIRIAM. I don't have any of those colors.

SARAH. What colors do you have?

MIRIAM. Green. And orange. And red. And blue. That's all. I left the rest of my crayons at Uncle Joseph and Aunt Mary's, in Bethlehem.

SARAH. *(thinking)* Which of those colors do you think would suit God best?

MIRIAM. Blue is supposed to be unhappy, isn't it? *(***SARAH*** nods.)* And red is for angry? When Uncle Joseph gets angry, he goes quite red.

SARAH. So you don't think those two are quite right, then?

MIRIAM. I thought about green, because that's the color of the trees and the grass. But I never saw a green person.

SARAH. No. You've never been to Ireland.

MIRIAM. *(ignoring a comment she doesn't understand)* That leaves only orange.

SARAH. Well, that would be a good color for God, actually. In Buddhist countries, they use orange as the color that holy people wear.

MIRIAM. *(tentatively wiggling in some orange lines)* It makes God a bit like the sun. I think I'll use orange –

(She's interrupted by the chimes on the door, the kind that tingaling every time someone uses the door. The three wise ones come in, looking very dusty and tired. **ISLAM** *has a small prayer mat, rolled up, under his arm.)*

ISLAM. *(bowing)* Good evening, madam and child.

HINDU. *(with praying gesture)* Namaste *(pronounced "Nah-MAHSS-teh")*

BUDDHIST. *(irritably to* **HINDU***)* Must you speak your native tongue in foreign countries? If English was good enough for the Christian Bible, it should be good enough for you. *(to* **SARAH** *and* **MIRIAM***)* Howdy do.

ISLAM. You will perhaps pardon our lack of civility,

HINDU. But it is a matter of some urgency.

BUDDHIST. Do this restaurant have restrooms?

(**SARAH** *gestures to the back. The three jostle each other in their hurry to get to the washrooms.*)

ALL THREE. I get it first!

No, me!

You were first last time! etc.

MIRIAM. Mom?

SARAH. Yes dear?

MIRIAM. Should I use the same color for God every time? Or could I use different colors?

SARAH. *(thoughtfully)* I think you could use different colors. Since no one has actually seen God – not since Moses, anyway, and Moses only saw God's backside…

MIRIAM. *(crayon poised, suddenly fascinated)* God has a bum?

(**SARAH** *opens her mouth to speak, but…the front door opens. The chimes herald the arrival of another person. A really imaginative director could have the chimes playing a different tune, depending on the character of the arriving person.*)

GUARD. Are those your camels outside there?

SARAH. Probably the three gents in the Gents. *(gestures towards the back)*

GUARD. Because they're tied up in a no-parking zone. I'm gonna have to give them a ticket. *(digs out his yellow pad of tickets, and licks the point of his pencil on his tongue)* Now let me see, what day is this?

MIRIAM. *(brightly)* It's the day after Christmas.

SARAH. "And all through the house

MIRIAM & SARAH. "not a creature was stirring, not even a –"

(*Sudden bedlam as the three wise ones emerge from the bathrooms.*)

HINDU. – a camel, I tell you!

ISLAM. A camel can carry enough water for a week inside itself. Often, while sojourning in the desert, I have –

BUDDHIST. But not even a camel ever had to go as badly as I did! I tell you, several times on that interminable ride up from the Jordan I would gladly have used my third wish for a convenient bush to hide behind!

ISLAM. You would have wasted our last wish on something as pathetic as a bush?

HINDU. In my country, people do not worry about such things. We have too much population–

ISLAM. I did not see you getting off to go stand by the side of the road.

HINDU. I did not want to attract the attention of the robbers.

ISLAM. *(shrugs)* If we are attacked, we are attacked. Inshallah.

BUDDHIST. *(to* **ISLAM***)* We would attract considerably less attention if you had not insisted in bringing all those ornate robes and carpets of yours. In my religion, we regard poverty and simplicity as virtues –

(While all this is going on, **SARAH** *pats* **MIRIAM** *on the head and sends her out to the kitchen.)*

GUARD. *(looking up from his ticket pad)* Are those your camels out there?

(The three wise ones immediately look around the restaurant to see if there is anyone else **GUARD** *could be speaking to. There is no one.* **SARAH** *looks at them and shrugs.)*

ISLAM. We have camels, of course.

HINDU. One each. That makes three.

GUARD. The ones tied up to the no-parking sign?

BUDDHIST. Ah! A riddle! Like the sound of one hand clapping, perhaps? If there is no parking, is a parked camel not parked, or –

GUARD. *(baffled and suddenly belligerent)* Listen, mister, don't start pulling fancy talk on me. I'm in charge here. His Herodian Majesty's Royal Constabulary and Parking Patrol. That's me, okay? You start playing smart with me, and we'll see who ends up looking out from behind bars –

ISLAM. Bars? I never touch the stuff!

HINDU. *(to* **SARAH***)* Is this place licensed? I could use a beer.

GUARD. *Prison* bars!

BUDDHIST. – if you can imagine it, as I was saying before I was so rudely interrupted, if you can *imagine* it, it is possible.

GUARD. *(looking suspicious)* Where are you folks from, anyway? You don't look like locals.

HINDU. We're not. As you can see,

BUDDHIST. He's from India,

HINDU. *(to no one in particular)* And my karma had better reincarnate me several steps up the ladder after traveling with these two!

ISLAM. And he's from Nepal.

HINDU. And the Ayatollah here is from Persia.

> *(If women play any of these parts, change the "he" to "she" appropriately.)*

GUARD. So you're strangers in these parts, are you?

ALL THREE. *(hopefully)* We are.

GUARD. Your camels are illegally parked. I have to give each of you a ticket. *(He starts tearing off the tickets.)*

ISLAM. I think I hear the call to prayer. You'll have to excuse me.

> *(He starts unrolling his prayer mat, turning around several times to determine which way is East, and eventually having to consult a pocket compass.)*

SARAH. Mecca? It's that way. *(pointing)*

ISLAM. Thank you.

BUDDHIST. *(kicking the mat away)* Get up, you hypocrite.

ISLAM. Be careful how you touch this priceless relic, godless infidel. It belonged to my great grandfather's cousin's uncle's brother.

HINDU. *(to* **GUARD***)* Five times a day he does this, and for some strange reason, he always needs to do it whenever we get into some difficulty.

(ISLAM *kneels on the floor, first looking up to heaven with his hands extended, as if expecting to receive something, then rocking forward to press his forehead to the ground.*)

GUARD. Let's see. Which camel is licence XJM 555, tattooed on its upper hip?

HINDU. The racy sports job? That's mine. Thank you.

GUARD. And NZF 608? With the limo on top?

BUDDHIST. His. (*Jerking his head contemptuously at* ISLAM. GUARD *drops the ticket into* ISLAM*'s cupped and outstretched hands.* ISLAM *looks at the ticket, astonished, then at heaven, and immediately redoubles the rate at which he prays.*)

BUDDHIST. It's not from God, silly. There is no God.

ISLAM. Correction. There is no God but God, whose name is Allah, and Mohammed is his prophet.

HINDU. (*drily*) There's one divine substance we call Brahman, and *everyone* makes a profit.

SARAH. (*aside*) My daughter thinks God is orange.

HINDU. Don't let any Irish Catholics hear you say that.

GUARD. (*ignoring all this byplay, hands the final ticket to* BUDDHIST) Therefore this one must be yours. (*to all three*) That will be 30 pieces of silver.

HINDU. (*gestures at* ISLAM, *still prostrating himself on the mat*) He has the money bag. You'll have to wait for him to finish.

GUARD. Nice carpet he's got there.

ISLAM. (*immediately stops bobbing and ducking*) You like it? Perhaps we could make an arrangement. Would you like a cup of tea?

SARAH. I'll get it. (*hurries off*)

ISLAM. You might, perhaps, like to see some of the carpets that I have on my camel. This one, this pathetic sample of the weaver's art, is but a fragment of the reflected glory of those outside which –

GUARD. The answer is no. I'm not taking any overpriced Persian prayer mats instead of your parking fines.

ISLAM. They are beautiful carpets.

HINDU. *(acidly)* Indeed they are. We have had to admire them across a thousand miles of desert!

GUARD. If you don't pay up, I'll have your camels towed. Then what good will your carpets do you?

BUDDHIST. That which is owing must be paid. Thirty pieces of silver.

ISLAM. Each?

GUARD. *(assimilating this wonderful idea)* Well, uh, *yes!* Seeing as you're strangers here, each! You can pay me now, or go directly to jail. Do not pass Go, and do not collect $200.

BUDDHIST. *(to* **ISLAM***)* You've got the gold.

HINDU. I do not think this man will accept a lump of frank-incense or a squirt of myrrh as payment.

ISLAM. Very well. I shall dispense the gold… if I can get into my money belt…

*(***ISLAM*** *starts digging through his voluminous robes. He gets his hand deep down inside where his money belt would be, and starts rooting around.)*

ISLAM. I know I had it once.

*(***SARAH*** *comes back in with a tea pot, closely followed my* ***MIRIAM*** *carrying tea cups. They stop in astonishment, watching* ***ISLAM*** *grope in his underwear.)*

MIRIAM. What's he doing, Mummy?

ISLAM. Ah, there it is.

*(***SARAH*** *hastily covers* ***MIRIAM****'s eyes.* ***ISLAM*** *wriggles his hand out, and holds in it a purse.)*

ISLAM. Thirty pieces of silver, you say. For the three of us, that would then be 90 pieces, almost one 24-karat gold coin. *(spills the purse of gold coins out onto the table)* Very well. I suppose it is one less gold coin for the King, that is all.

GUARD. The King? What king?

HINDU & BUDDHIST. The King we have come to see, of course.

GUARD. *(digesting this new idea)* You've come to see the King?

ISLAM. Do we look like we've come to see the Wizard of Oz?

GUARD. *(suddenly most obsequious)* My apologies, gentlemen. I had no idea. Royal visitors are, of course, exempt from parking regulations. Diplomatic immunity, they call it. Please. Forgive me. Allow me to destroy those tickets...

(The three stare at each other, like stout Balboa upon a peak in Darien, stricken with a wild surmise. They turn as one, holding their tickets close to them.)

ALL THREE. No!

GUARD. But –

BUDDHIST. We will not release them!

HINDU. Our human rights as royal visitors have been violated. We appeal to the king.

BUDDHIST. A word once spoken cannot be recalled.

ISLAM. The king himself must come and invalidate these tickets.

SARAH. The King? Coming here? My God...Miriam, go get Rachel! Quick!

MIRIAM. *(scuttling out to the kitchen calling)* Rachel! Rachel! The king is coming!

HINDU. If he does not come, we shall take this clear case of racial prejudice to your Civil Liberties Association.

GUARD. I will see. I will see...

(GUARD hurries out the door, taking a vicious kick at what he thinks is a camel. The "camel" tries to bite him and he recoils appropriately.)

GUARD. Back, you overgrown goat! May the fleas of a thousand Arabs infest your armpits, all four of them....

RACHEL. *(hustling in, with MIRIAM at her heels)* Did you say the King is coming here?

ALL THREE. We believe so.

RACHEL. Sarah! Sarah, we've got to get rid of these cockroaches before he gets here or we'll lose our licence for sure. Sarah!

(RACHEL, MIRIAM and SARAH immediately set about a search and destroy mission, punctuating their search with cries of "There's one!" "Get him!" They stamp their feet vigorously, squishing whatever it is they can find.)

HINDU. Ah, flamenco dancing!

ISLAM. I trust there is no cover charge for the entertainment.

RACHEL. *(chasing one which scuttles under the cloaks of the three wise ones)* You – lift your feet!

(HINDU lifts one foot.)

RACHEL. It's not there. Lift the other foot.

HINDU. Alas, I have not yet reached that exalted level in yoga meditation in which I am able to levitate.

(BUDDHIST and ISLAM take an arm each, and lift him off the floor.)

HINDU. *(dusts off his arms)* I appreciate your efforts to help – but it is not the same as levitation.

MIRIAM. *(on the floor, bum up, peering under feet)* It's not there.

RACHEL. It must have gone under one of the other of you.

(BUDDHIST and ISLAM raise their feet alternately, while MIRIAM scuttles around them on her hands and knees.)

RACHEL. Get off the floor, all of you. Here – up onto the tables! Get up there!

(SARAH sweeps the candles off the tables, and sets them, and all the silverware, hastily on the table nearest the front of the stage. The three wise ones hop dutifully up onto the three remaining tables. They sit cross legged, BUDDHIST and HINDU in the lotus position, or as close to it as they can manage, ISLAM in a more conventional leg-crossing.)

ISLAM. *(poking SARAH with his toe as she passes)* Give me my prayer mat, O flower of the forest.

SARAH. Get it yourself, buster. Next you'll be wanting a loaf a bread, and a jug of wine.

HINDU. So far, I haven't even seen a menu!

MIRIAM. I'll get one, Mom. *(runs out)*

ISLAM. What a good idea! A loaf of bread, a glass of wine... We have not had a good glass of wine, since, when was it now?

HINDU. Damascus.

BUDDHIST. No, Baghdad.

ISLAM. That was not good wine in Baghdad. They made it with local water.

BUDDHIST. That bottle you picked up in Damascus wasn't so hot either. You pulled the cork and out popped a genie.

ISLAM. And what did *he* wish for? *(waving blindly at* **HINDU***)* A case of Scotch whisky!

HINDU. Whereupon *you* immediately wished that I would perform an anatomical impossibility upon myself. I found myself in a yoga position that no one had previously attempted, and from which it took me two days to extricate myself.

BUDDHIST. Which was just about how long it took you *(to* **ISLAM***)* to finish the Scotch.

ISLAM. *(sanctimoniously)* Alcohol has never touched my lips. It is forbidden, by the Qu'ran.

BUDDHIST. You used a straw! You've probably still got it!

ISLAM. Of course. I've got it right here! *(plucks an oversized straw out from under his robes)* One must not question the wily wisdom of the prophet. *(suddenly irritated)* So where is that jug of wine and loaf of bread, wench?

SARAH. *(sweeping up the last of the crushed roaches)* Your dinner will be along in just a minute, sir. The kitchen is very busy tonight.

*(***RACHEL*** looks up in astonishment.)*

SARAH. *(shrugs)* Well, isn't that what waitresses always say?

RACHEL. You're learning. Now if I could teach you Galilean peasants which side the knives and forks go on...

BUDDHIST. Well, personally, I wish –

HINDU & ISLAM. Stop!

ISLAM. We only have one wish left. Don't waste it on something frivolous!

(fanfare offstage)

GUARD. *(voice offstage)* Out of the way, you misbegotten creation of a committee!

(Door opens; chimes ring. The **CLERK** *comes in, blowing a fanfare on a kazoo. He is followed by the* **GUARD.** **HEROD** *sleazes his way into the restaurant.)*

KING. All clear?

GUARD. Ten-four, your majesty.

KING. No lurking assassins?

GUARD. *(checks under the tables)* None, your highness.

BUDDHIST. *(nervously)* Ommm.

(He keeps this chant up until stopped to speak. **HINDU** *does deep breathing exercises as audibly as possible.)*

KING. My usual table.

RACHEL. *(hastily)* I'm afraid it's, umm, occupied this evening, your magnificence.

KING. So I see. *(gives barely a glance at the figure squatting on the table)* Then I'll take my other usual table.

RACHEL. *(glancing at the three bodies perched upon tables)* They're also, uh, occupied at the moment. But we set this table especially for you, your beneficence. As you can see, we provided it with four candles, yes indeed, four, one-two-three-four…

GUARD. *(gruffly)* And enough cutlery for a small army. What's going on here?

RACHEL. Occasionally, his exaltedness travels with a small army.

GUARD. Why *four* candles?

RACHEL. *(desperately)* It's because of the, uh, twelve tribes of Israel of which, ah, er, – *(The rest of the explanation follows in a breathless non-stop string.)*

SARAH. – of which but two now remain, Israel and Judah, over the southern of which your high-and-mightiness now reigns, which leaves but one –

RACHEL. – but because our ancestor Jacob, who was married to my namesake Rachel, whose tomb this is, may God rest her soul, and Rachel was one of two sisters –

HINDU. – which added to the one makes three –

BUDDHIST. – multiplied by the original twelve tribes is 36 –

ISLAM. – from which you subtract the seven days of creation to make 29 –

SARAH. – less the day on which God rested is 28 –

HINDU. – divided by the number of the days of the week is four. So, four candles. Simple, is it not?

(KING *looks baffled, and is about to take a seat when* SARAH *snatches it away from him and swats a cockroach on the seat. She hands the chair back to him with a smile.*)

KING. *(glancing at an occupied table)* I see you've started selling souvenir smiling Buddhas on the side, Rachel. Have you paid your licence fee as a retail sales operation yet?

(CLERK *hastily pulls a clipboard from his satchel full of papers and scrolls, scrabbles through his clipboard, looks up, starts shaking his head and opens his/her mouth to say No but doesn't have time.*)

KING. Have you paid your quarterly income tax installments on time?

(CLERK *scrabbles through clipboard again, same routine.*)

KING. Have my extortion boys been here yet?

(CLERK *scrabbles yet again, this time smilingly nods.* RACHEL *simulataneously grimaces and nods.*)

KING. *(beaming at last)* Good!

RACHEL. Begging your pardon, your beatitude, this is still just a humble non-profit restaurant, not a souvenir shop. These, your omnipotence, are visitors from far-off lands.

HINDU. India.

BUDDHIST. Burma.

ISLAM. Persia, or as we prefer to call it, Iran.

RACHEL. They have just arrived in the kingdom of Judah.

BUDDHIST. Judah?

ISLAM. Is that the king's name?

HINDU. The one whom we seek?

KING. *(thunderously)* No!

CLERK. The king's name is Herod.

GUARD. *(threateningly)* And don't you forget it.

HINDU. The kingdom is named after someone other than the king? Who is this greater being, this ultimate other?

KING. *(furious)* There is no greater other. I am the king. I am the king. I am the king! *("I am the king" becomes a pathetic refrain.)*

BUDDHIST. We heard you the first time – all three of us.

ISLAM. Then who is Judah?

CLERK. He was – if your awesomeness will permit – the son of one of the two sisters who became the father of one of the twelve tribes, before ten of them were lost.

HINDU. *(slapping his thigh in delight)* The answer is 42! I knew it!

KING. *(like a cracked record)* I am the king! I am the king!

BUDDHIST. *(unmoved, fearlessly button-nosing him)* But you are not the king we seek.

KING. I am the only king in Judah.

CLERK. That is true. He has – may it please your depravity – he has exterminated all his brothers and sisters so that there could be no other contender for the throne.

KING. I am the king!

GUARD. And you better remember that!

> *(As this goes on, **MIRIAM** comes to the kitchen door with her menu, and then sits there, watching, but not taking part.)*

HINDU. Why should we bother remembering a two-bit tax collector?

ISLAM. An extortionist.

BUDDHIST. A petty tyrant *(brushing something out from under his robes)* who crushes his people like cockroaches.

(SARAH hastily stamps on whatever it was that he brushed out from under his robes, and pretends she hadn't done anything as she scuffs it under the table with her foot.)

KING. *(beaming Sally Fields-like)* They know me!

ISLAM. *(dead serious now)* No.

BUDDHIST. *(also serious)* If you are a king....

(RACHEL, SARAH, CLERK, and GUARD all crowd around with looks of wonder on their faces)

then we seek a different king.

KING, SARAH, RACHEL, CLERK, & GUARD. A different king?

KING. There is no other king! I am the king! I am the king! *(His voice unaccountably cracks on the final words.)*

ALL THREE. There is another king.

KING. Nonsense! Do you think I was born yesterday?

(The three get off their tables and come closer. They open KING's mouth, examine his teeth like a horse, feel his jowls, check his paunch... then respond thoughtfully.)

BUDDHIST. No.

HINDU. Definitely not yesterday.

ISLAM. But the king we seek *was* born yesterday.

KING. I am the king....

RACHEL. Please don't upset him. It could be very bad for my business.

KING. *(His voice is almost a croak.)* Yesterday?

HINDU. That is so, according to the stars. We are experts in reading the signs of the universe. Our ancient manuscripts foretold the coming of a prince of peace, a wonderful counsellor, of the very being and nature of God –

ISLAM. Even though there is no God but Allah and Muhammed is –

HINDU. …of the *being* and nature of God, incarnated as a human, who will be born on this earth. And I –

BUDDHIST. – We –

HINDU. – have each –

ISLAM. – independently –

HINDU. – observed the conjunctions of the stars which told us that this event would come to pass.

ISLAM. We have traveled many months from our respective countries.

BUDDHIST. We met along the way, each of us pursuing the stars –

ISLAM. – independently –

HINDU. Each night, the stars that hold the destiny of kings have drawn closer together.

ISLAM. Last night, in the clear cold night of the desert

BUDDHIST. – three trees on a ridge silhouetted against the last gleam of the sunset –

HINDU. – as we sat by our campfire, with the earth balanced within the orb of the heavens –

BUDDHIST. – we saw *(awed)*…

ISLAM. …the stars!

HINDU. …the stars came together!

BUDDHIST. They formed a new star, a brighter constellation….

ISLAM. A star is born!

(Sudden silence. Offstage, a rooster crows.)

KING. *(Briefly terror-stricken, the king now breaks the silence by clapping his hands.)* Wonderful! Great performance! Haha! Hahaha! Hahahahahahahahaha! *(to* **CLERK***)* Give 'em a tip and toss 'em out.

*(***SARAH** *and* **RACHEL***, taking their cue from the King, first applaud and then fall silent again.* **RACHEL** *starts to shoo the wise ones out.)*

CLERK. *(weaselling)* Perhaps, if it please your brutalitiness, you should not dismiss them too quickly. There is, in our archives, a certain legend…

KING. Legend? What legend?

CLERK. *(flipping through the pages)* That a root from the stump of Jesse shall spring up, and he shall be called Prince of Peace, and Mighty Counsellor, and the government of the nations shall be upon his head. Perhaps, your excruciatingness, if you were to question them further…?

KING. *(with dawning awareness)* Ahem!

*(**WISE ONES** stop on their way to the door.)*

KING. *(suddenly oozing charm)* Rachel, my dear, this is hardly Middle Eastern hospitality. You should make these strangers happy. *(to **CLERK**)* What is that our scriptures say about strangers?

CLERK. *(quoting)* "You shall befriend the widow and the orphan and the stranger in your midst – subject of course to your autocracy's pleasure – for you were yourselves once strangers in the land of Egypt."

KING. I know. I got ripped off by a taxi driver in Cairo. You should see the way those idiots drive….

CLERK. Moses also complained.

KING. They had taxis in Moses' day?

GUARD. *(lugubriously)* You can't give parking tickets to taxis.

KING. Rachel! Why haven't you fed these good folks? Bring them what they want!

RACHEL. Who's paying for this?

KING. They are, of course.

ISLAM. We had already placed our order…

SARAH. I know, I know, a loaf of bread, a jug of wine….

*(**SARAH** hastens off.)*

KING. *(making conversation)* So, uh, how long have you guys been on the road?

BUDDHIST. I think that I've come the farthest. Took me about 40 weeks.

KING. Is it difficult travelling this time of year?

HINDU. Only coming through Afghanistan.

BUDDHIST. They were at war with each other.

HINDU. Again.

KING. (*to* **ISLAM**) And where did you meet up with them, then?

ISLAM. In the hospital.

BUDDHIST. Montezuma's revenge.

HINDU. We made the mistake of drinking the water in Mesopotamia.

ISLAM. If that was really the Garden of Eden, Adam and Eve would have died drinking that stuff.

SARAH. (*offstage*) Miriam, you bring the jug of wine, please. (*enters carrying a loaf of fresh baked bread*)

KING. (*leering, having disposed of the pleasantries*) So tell me just where is this new king right now?

(**MIRIAM** *enters with a jug of wine.* **SARAH** *sets it on the King's table.*)

KING. (*sniffs the jug of wine, and snorts*) Pooh. Rotgut!

RACHEL. (*gesturing at* **SARAH**) What can you expect? It came from Cana in Galilee.

CLERK. Near Nazareth.

GUARD. (*scornfully*) Can anything good come out of Nazareth?

KING. (*quaffing directly from the jug of rotgut and banging it down on the table*) So. Where is he right now?

ISLAM. (*digs out an antique pocket watch and peers at it*) Since he was born just 24 hours ago, I would guess he's sleeping.

BUDDHIST. Or suckling at his mother's breast, perhaps.

KING. Where?

HINDU. That is the problem. We do not know for sure. We are simply following the stars, and now that they have begun to come apart again... (*He shrugs.*)

KING. Somewhere near here, then?

BUDDHIST. Probably.

KING. (*to* **CLERK.**) You – you were quoting that stuff about the stump of Jesse. Where'd you get that stuff from?

CLERK. May it please your loathsomeness, it was the prophet Isaiah.

KING. What else does he have to say?

CLERK. About 63 chapters. No offence meant to your vituperativeness, but he is one of the more long-winded of the prophets.

KING. *(impatiently)* Where does the old windbag say this shoot is going to sprout?

(CLERK goes into a paroxysm of searching through papers and scrolls, and drops one which rolls across the floor. MIRIAM helps him retrieve it. He pats her on the head and starts to read.)

CLERK. He doesn't, specifically. But this is close. "But thou, Bethlehem, in the land of Judah, are by no means the least among the rulers of Judah, for out of you shall come a ruler who will rule my people Israel."

MIRIAM. Bethlehem, Mommy. That's where we live, isn't it?

(SARAH shushes MIRIAM.)

KING. Where in Bethlehem?

CLERK. It doesn't say, your ambivalence. When this was written, they didn't have any street addresses.

KING. That's not much help. *(to wise ones)* And you don't have any idea which house or family this might be?

(The three look sheepish.)

KING. *(disgusted)* All right, I'll tell you what I'll do. Because you're strangers here, I won't charge you with anything.

(The three throw their parking tickets in the air.)

But I need you to do me a favor.

(The three bow.)

KING. *(with an ingratiating leer)* I want you to go through Bethlehem, and see if you can find this child that you say has been born. If you can find him, y'all come back here, y'see, and y'all tell me all about it. Because if this kid is half as special as you say, then I'd kind of like to go and see him myself.

(The three bow again.)

KING. *(aside, to* **GUARD**) And you follow them, and let me know where they go.

GUARD. Right. If they park those camels anywhere, I've got 'em, chief!

KING. Good to meet you folks. Hope to see you again real soon now. God bless y'all.

*(***CLERK*** *bows and scrapes, the* **GUARD** *holds the door open, the* **KING** *sweeps through it like a dustball blowing away.)*

MIRIAM. I didn't like that man. I don't trust him.

SARAH. Hush, child, you can't say that about him.

BUDDHIST. Why not? It's true. I didn't like him either.

HINDU. I would not trust that guy as far as I could throw an elephant.

RACHEL. He's mixed blood, you know. Not really pure Jewish stock.

MIRIAM. *(has scuttled over to the door and peered through)* That other man, the big one – he hasn't gone?

ISLAM. No. He's staying to spy on us. He'll probably follow us when we leave here. I recognize the trick. I've used it on dissidents in my own country.

BUDDHIST. When the waters grow calmer, the mirror grows clearer. We all recognize ourselves in these events.

(long pause)

BUDDHIST. Well, we've come a long way to be frustrated in our quest by a local sleazebag.

HINDU. If we find the child, certainly that man will execute him. And that will not be good for the child's health.

ISLAM. So it's over, then. Our great journey.

BUDDHIST. I think so. Yes, I'm afraid so. Y'know, I wish it weren't…

(another pause)

HINDU. Now you've done it.

BUDDHIST. Done what?

HINDU. Used up the last wish. Not that it matters much, at this point.

ISLAM. I cannot claim that this trip has been a pleasure. The worst time of the year for a journey, and such a long journey....

BUDDHIST. ...the cities hostile, the towns unfriendly....

HINDU. ...the villages dirty, and charging high prices.

ISLAM. A hard time we had of it. Our camels galled, sore-footed, refractory

HINDU. There have been times I regretted this trip.

ISLAM. I missed the summer palaces on slopes, the terraces, the silken girls....

BUDDHIST. Were we led all this way for birth, or death?

HINDU. There was a birth, certainly.

ISLAM. Yes, but this birth has been like a death for me.

BUDDHIST. Me too. I thought we were led here to celebrate the coming of life. Instead I have this terrible sense of ending.

ISLAM. Allah forgive me, but I will not be able to think again of you people who worship other gods as mere infidels. You may not worship the one true God, but your faith has stood you well during this trying time. When we return to our places, I too shall no longer be at ease among an alien people clutching their narrow gods....

HINDU. We Hindus are not narrow at all. We have gods for everyone. Plenty of gods and plenty types of gods. Still, I have to say, *Moksha*. I see now the liberating force of having just one God who draws near and becomes real for people. It is, you may say, satisfactory.

BUDDHIST. We Buddhists do not believe in God at all. Pure, unchanging, impersonal spirit. That's all you get from Brahman and from it flows nothing but maya, illusion, deception. Still, I can't help thinking that something other than fate has brought us here together....

HINDU. Good friends. Please. The time has come. Take and eat.

(HINDU takes the loaf, and breaks it. He passes it to the other two wise ones, and to MIRIAM and SARAH and RACHEL. They eat in silence. ISLAM then takes the jug, and pours some glasses of wine.)

ISLAM. In the name of Allah, the Compassionate, the Merciful.

(The others lift their glasses and look to him. He hesitates, and then remembers his straw. He pulls it out and sticks it into the glass ready to use it.)

BUDDHIST. Cheer up! It can't be all that bad if we're eating and drinking together. Better anyway than killing each other. *(looking up)* Thank you.

(They raise their glasses.)

BUDDHIST. To the child we seek.

HINDU. To the child in all of us.

ISLAM. To all the children of God.

(They drink.)

MIRIAM. Did you mean that, about the baby being born just yesterday?

(The three nod.)

MIRIAM. Aunt Mary's baby was born just yesterday. Wasn't he, Mom?

SARAH. Yes, he was.

BUDDHIST. *(idly)* Where?

SARAH. *(gushing)* In a stable, just down the road here, in Bethlehem. We came down with them for the census. From their home in Nazareth. Cousin Mary knew she was going to have a baby, and wondered if Miriam could stay with them to baby sit the boy. I don't know how she knew it was going to be a boy. But she was sure. I think she even said something about an angel telling her.

(RACHEL laughs; the others snicker a little.)

MIRIAM. Mom! Mom, do you think it could be Mary's little boy?

SARAH. What could?

MIRIAM. The baby that they're looking for?

SARAH. Who's looking for?

MIRIAM. *(pointing to the three wise ones)* Them!

SARAH. A baby born in a stable, a king? Oh come on, Miriam, you have a great imagination, but...

MIRIAM. *(excitedly)* But it could be, Mom. Really, it could be.

HINDU. Maybe we should – how do they say it around here in Yiddish? – check it out.

ISLAM. What have we got to lose?

BUDDHIST. Our heads, that's what. What about that guy standing outside watching our camels?

MIRIAM. There's a back way. I could take you there. It's just a short walk, over the hills and down the ridge. The shepherds do it easily. Oh, please! Please come.

RACHEL. *(doubtfully)* I suppose I could go out and distract that man for a while...

ISLAM. Yeah, we can forget the animals. I still have the gold. *(rummaging around in his robes)*

HINDU. I have the frankincense with me.

BUDDHIST. And I the myrrh.

HINDU. The gifts matter; nothing else does. We have done with nothing before; we can do with nothing again. Let this Herod character have our camels.

BUDDHIST. Our prayer scrolls.

ISLAM. *(more regretfully)* My carpets.

MIRIAM. *(excitedly)* Come on. It's him. I'm sure it is. Come on!

HINDU. All right. Let's go.

ISLAM. Wait! What about this meal? We haven't paid for it!

RACHEL. It's on the house....

> *(MIRIAM leads off through any otherwise unused exit, RACHEL goes to the door where the GUARD's shadow hulks against the glass, hesitates, and opens it. The others go off to the rear, following MIRIAM, suddenly feeling hopeful again.)*

THE MOUSE'S DISCOVERY

A Christmas Pageant for Children of All Ages

by Marion McTavish

CAST

(reading parts)
HEAD PALACE MOUSE
HEAD MAGI MOUSE
HEAD FIELD MOUSE
HEAD STABLE MOUSE

(miming parts)
KING HEROD
MAGI *
PALACE MICE *
SHEPHERDS *
FIELD MICE *
ANGELS *
JOSEPH
MARY
BABY

* can be any number or sex

SET

A lectern stands on one side of the stage where the Head Palace Mouse sits, and a pulpit stands on the other side where the Head Field Mouse sits. On the far side of the lectern is a large throne on which King Herod sits. Just beyond this is a Christmas tree. Across the back, between the lectern and the pulpit, is the choir loft or elevated chairs on which the Angels sit.

The first verse of familiar Christmas songs will be sung throughout the presentation. The audience is invited to remain seated and join in the singing.

The suggested songs include: "Deck the Halls," "We Three Kings," "It Came Upon the Midnight Clear," "While Shepherds Watched Their Flocks by Night," "Angels We Have Heard on High," "We Three Kings of Orient Are," "O Come All Ye Faithful," "Away in a Manger," "Joy to the World, " and "Silent Night."

(KING HEROD is sitting on his throne and the PALACE MICE are decorating the Christmas tree while the audience sings the first verse of "Deck the Halls." As the song ends, the PALACE MICE scamper to the lectern and sit on the floor looking up at the HEAD PALACE MOUSE as he/she speaks.)

HEAD PALACE MOUSE. It is with great joy that I accept your vote of confidence in me as Head Palace Mouse. My family is getting settled here in our new home, and I must say we are pleased. This palace has everything! It is far superior to any other place in Jerusalem. Sharing the facilities with King Herod and his family has its ups and downs, but I am sure we will manage.

(pointing to the back)

Wait a minute. Who are those strangers outside the palace? They must be newcomers to Jerusalem. Hmm. I better send out some mice to find out who they are. *(beckoning to PALACE MICE)* Palace Mice! Find out who those strangers are.

(PALACE MICE scamper to the back where the MAGI and the HEAD MAGI MOUSE are waiting.)

SONG " WE THREE KINGS"

(During the singing of "We Three Kings," the PALACE MICE lead the MAGI and HEAD MAGI MOUSE slowly up the aisle where they stand in front of Herod's throne. The PALACE MICE return to the lectern and sit in front of it.)

HEAD PALACE MOUSE. Hello! Hello! Excuse me. You seem to be new to these parts. Who are you? What are you looking for? Why are you here in Jerusalem?

HEAD MAGI MOUSE. Are you speaking to me?

HEAD PALACE MOUSE. Yes, I am! Who are you?

HEAD MAGI MOUSE. I am a mouse.

HEAD PALACE MOUSE. I can see that. But you're not from these parts. What tribe are you from?

HEAD MAGI MOUSE. I am the Head Magi Mouse. I live with the Magi. They are wise and learned people. We are following the star.

HEAD PALACE MOUSE. But why have you come to Herod's Palace?

HEAD MAGI MOUSE. We are searching for the new baby who is going to be the king of the Jews.

HEAD PALACE MOUSE. A new baby is going to be the king of the Jews? I'm not sure Herod will like this. He thinks HE is the king of the Jews. And you say a new king is about to be born? I smell trouble brewing.

(**KING HEROD** *has been listening to this dialogue and becomes increasingly angry. Then he has an idea. He stands up, smiles and holds out his arms as if to welcome the people to his palace.*)

HEAD PALACE MOUSE. *(interpreting Herod's miming gestures)* What? No kidding! A dinner party? Right here in this palace? Wow! That's great! And everybody is invited. Even the magi. That's even better. I've got to gather all the Palace Mice. The pickings are going to be awesome. If our poor country cousins had any idea!

(*All sit and the* **HEAD FIELD MOUSE** *jumps up to the pulpit.*)

HEAD FIELD MOUSE. Hi. Someone call me? I keep hearing these strange sounds. It's usually so quiet in the fields at night. That's why I love being a field mouse. The shepherds are always so generous. They share their food with us. And the sheep even let us have pieces of wool to line our nests.

The city critters wonder what we do for entertainment out here in the country. But they have no idea what it's like to sit around the campfire at night with the shepherds and listen to the jokes and laughter. There is something strange in the air tonight, though. Don't you sense it? Listen. I hear something.

SONG, " IT CAME UPON THE MIDNIGHT CLEAR"

(As the song is sung, the **ANGELS** *stand up on their chairs or risers. The* **SHEPHERDS** *walk slowly up the aisle to the front where they sit on the floor looking up at the* **ANGELS**.*)*

HEAD FIELD MOUSE. There's something very special about this night. I can just feel it. I think we had better have a country council meeting and check this out. Field Mice! Country Mice! Deer Mice!

(The **FIELD MICE** *begin scampering from the back of the church or auditorium. Some of them crawl under the pews – with electrifying effects! When they get to the front they sit with the* **SHEPHERDS**. *While the* **FIELD MICE** *are "scampering," the* **HEAD FIELD MOUSE** *continues talking.)*

We are having a mouse meeting and you are all invited. Check with the shepherds on your way to the meeting and see if you can gather any news.

SONG, "WHILE SHEPHERDS WATCHED THEIR FLOCKS BY NIGHT"

(During the song the **ANGELS**, *who have been standing on their chairs, lift their arms towards the* **SHEPHERDS** *in the form of a blessing.)*

HEAD FIELD MOUSE. I knew there was something different about this night. Angels! Real angels! Did you hear what they said? "Fear not: for behold, I bring you good tidings of great joy, which shall be to all people. For unto you is born this day in the city of David, a Saviour, which is Christ the Lord. And this shall be a sign unto you; ye shall find the babe wrapped in swaddling clothes, lying in a manger."

SONG, "ANGELS WE HAVE HEARD ON HIGH"

(At song's end, **ANGELS** *sit down.)*

HEAD FIELD MOUSE. "Let us now go even unto Bethlehem, and see this thing which is come to pass, which the Lord has made known unto us."

(HEAD FIELD MOUSE *leads* SHEPHERDS *and* FIELD MICE *down the aisle to the back.*)

PALACE MOUSE. *(at lectern)* What a feast! And King Herod still didn't get what he was after. The scribes and priests had no idea where this new king of the Jews could be found. And so the next day Herod invited the magi to his palace and said to them…

(HEROD *stands and mimes.*)

"Go to Bethlehem and make a careful search for the child; and when you find him, let me know; so that I too may go and worship him."

When the wise men left the palace the huge bright star that has been in the sky these last few nights was still shining bright and sparkly. The wise men seem to be following it. Maybe we should go with them.

SONG, CHORUS OF "WE THREE KINGS"

(*During the song, the* PALACE MOUSE *leads the* MAGI, *the* HEAD MAGI, *and* THE PALACE MICE *slowly down the center aisle to the back.* HEROD, *meanwhile, quietly exits.*)

STABLE MOUSE. *(running up to the pulpit from the back)* Wow! Did you hear the news? I'm so excited I can't stand still. Everyone is coming here to Bethlehem. The streets are going to be packed with people. And you know what that means. Where there's people, there's food. And where there's food… *(rubs his stomach)*

But let me introduce myself. I am the Stable Mouse and I live here in these stables. I used to live in the inn over there. They have lots of people that live there and, as you know, where there's people, there's food!

It was paradise…until – the innkeeper got a *cat!* That's when I realized it was time for me to get lost. There was no room in the inn.

(JOSEPH, who has been sitting in the front row, now walks slowly to the back. He stops frequently to mime – pleading for a room.)

STABLE MOUSE. *(cont.)* So I moved out here to the stable. Not many PEOPLE come out here, but I've made friends with all the animals. We work together and eat together and everyone is happy. Do you know the nicest thing about living in a stable? No one ever complains about not having enough room. There's always room for one more. Speaking of which – who is that?

(STABLE MOUSE goes to center front, watches JOSEPH for a moment, and then yells…)

Joseph! Joseph!! You can stay here. We've got lots of room!!!

(JOSEPH doesn't seem to hear and continues moving to the back of the auditorium/church. STABLE MOUSE returns to the pulpit.)

Don't get discouraged, Joseph. You can stay here. Bring Mary with you. The animals will keep you warm.

(HEAD FIELD MOUSE and HEAD PALACE MOUSE enter from back and start scampering up the center aisle.)

He doesn't hear me. We've got to help them. *(spots mice)* Who are you? You look like the Palace Mouse from Kind Herod's palace in Jerusalem. And you look like the Field Mouse that lives with the shepherds. Do you want to help? Sure you can help. Go and bring Mary and Joseph here. They can't find any room in the inn, but we can keep them warm and comfortable out here. Oh yes, and bring the magi and shepherds, too. Mary and Joseph are going to have a little baby. It's time for all of us to celebrate!

SONG, "O COME ALL YE FAITHFUL"

(During the song, all the actors come up to the front and stand in a semi-circle. A stool and manger are brought in for MARY, JOSEPH and the BABY).

SONG, "AWAY IN A MANGER"

(**MARY**, **JOSEPH** and the **BABY** walk slowly to the front, led by the **HEAD FIELD MOUSE** and the **HEAD PALACE MOUSE**.)

SONG, "JOY TO THE WORLD"

SONG, "SILENT NIGHT"

(If the pageant is performed in the context of a worship service, the following Benediction may be used.)

FIELD MOUSE. I'm only a little field mouse, but Jesus has made me important.

PALACE MOUSE. I may be a palace mouse but Jesus taught me the true meaning of humility.

STABLE MOUSE. As the stable mouse I was as close to Jesus as anybody. But now I know the real secret of the gospel.

FIELD MOUSE. We're all close to Jesus!

PALACE MOUSE. And Jesus is close to us all.

STABLE MOUSE. May his spirit be with you this Christmas and may God's love never let you go.

ALL THREE MICE. Amen!!!

THE GOOD SAMARITAN

by Richard Coleman

Introduction

One day Jesus was tested with this question: "If I am supposed to love my neighbour as myself, who is my neighbour?" Jesus answered by telling a story – the story that I am going to tell you now in pantomime. I invite you to join me by being an echo, repeating the same words and the same actions after me. Are you ready? Here we go!

I am who I am *(point to yourself)*.

One day I put on my sandals *(pretend to put on sandals)*.

And my traveling cloak *(mimic slipping arms into loose cloak)*.

I took my money bag *(hold imaginary bag in fist)*,

And hid it in my belt *(mimic tucking it in wide belt)*.

Then I started on my way *(walk in place)*

From Jerusalem to Jericho *(sweep arm in wide arc)*,

Uphill and downhill *(walking on the spot, leaning backward and then forward)*,

Past dark caves where robbers night hide *(shoulders hunched, palms straight out, fearful look)*

I pretended I wasn't afraid *(stand straight, big smile, hands clasped behind back)*;

But all of a sudden I was surrounded by robbers *(arms go up)*,

And one of them hit me *(crouch down, hands in front of face to ward off blows)*;

That was the last thing I remember *(bend down even further)*.

After a while *(cup hand to ear)*

I heard footsteps *(cross arms, slap hands on arms, begin standing again)*.

The footsteps grew louder *(slap more loudly)*.

It was a priest *(stop slapping; hold arms akimbo)*.

He said, "Can't stop now, sonny" *(look down and shake head, speaking sorrowfully)*,

"But I'll come back later" *(wave good-bye)*.

After a while *(cup hand to ear)*,

I heard new footsteps *(raise hands to shoulder level and snap fingers)*.

It was a Levite *(continue snapping fingers)*.

He said, "Too bad, too bad" *(stop finger snapping, shake head and speak with high squeaky voice)*;

Then he went on his way *(wave good-bye)*.

Soon I heard other footsteps *(slap thighs, one after the other)*.

It was a Samaritan on a donkey *(continue thigh-slapping)*.

"Whoa! Need any help?" *(mimic pulling reins, lean over and look down)*;

Then he jumped down *(jump up and down once)*,

And took off his cloak *(mimic taking off cloak)*,

Tore it into strips *(pretend to tear strips of cloth)*,

And bandaged my wounds *(mimic rolling bandages on wounded areas)*.

He lifted me onto his donkey *(mimic lifting and placing body gently)*,

And slowly we went on our way *(slap thighs more slowly)*,

Until we came to an inn – "Whoa!" *(mimic pulling back on reins)*

He carried me inside *(arms outstretched in carrying position)*,

And laid me on a bed *(pretend to place body on bed)*.

"Here is some money," he said to the innkeeper *(mimic taking coins from bag, speaking with deep gruff voice)*;

"I will pay all that is owed " *(pretend to tuck money bag back in belt)*.

Then he went on his way *(slowly slap thighs)*.

Now I ask you *(point finger at listeners while they of course point back at you)*,

Which one loved me as a neighbor *(point as if to three distinct persons)*:

The priest who said, "Can't stop now, sonny"? *(hold arms akimbo, shake head)*;

The Levite who said, "Too bad, too bad"? *(snap fingers)*;

Or the Good Samaritan? *(slap hands on thigh)*.

Go thou *(point to one side of the congregation)*,

And do likewise *(swing arm to other side of congregation)*.

This time we'll retell the story of the Good Samaritan as Jesus might have told it to us today. We'll speed the story up a little, and now that you have a feeling for the way the story will be told you might like to make your actions even more vigorous.

(Note to the leader: However much you speed the story up and even ham it up, make sure you slow the last two lines down so the point of the parable can really hit people – including oneself – between the eyeballs.)

I am who I am *(point to yourself)*.

One day I put on my shoes *(pretend to put on shoes)*.

And my leather jacket *(mimic slipping arms into jacket)*.

I took my money *(open hand)*

And hid it in my jeans pocket *(slip hand into back pocket)*.

Then I got on my ten-speed racer *(imitate climbing on bike)*,

And started on my way *(walk in place)*

From ——— to ——— (*name two local communities while walking in place and indicating the towns with sweeping hand motion*),

Uphill and downhill (*lean forward and then backward while still walking*),

Past big trees where muggers might hide (*stop walking and look fearful*),

I pretended I wasn't afraid (*stand straight, hands clasped behind back*).

But all of a sudden (*arms go up*),

The muggers jumped out at me (*jump back in fear, hands face out*)!

One of them hit me (*head to one side as if taking a blow*);

That was the last thing I remember (*bend head down*).

After a while (*cup hand to ear and bring head up*)

I heard footsteps (*cross arms, slapping hands on arms*).

The footsteps became louder (*slap more loudly and faster*).

It was a.....................minister (*name your own denomination; stop slapping and hold arms akimbo*)

He said, "Can't stop now, sonny" (*look down and shake head, speaking very piously*)

I've got an important.................to attend (*name important committee in your church*)

"But I'll come back later." (*wave good-bye*).

After a while (*cup hand to ear*),

I heard new footsteps (*raise hands to shoulder level, snap fingers*).

It was a school teacher from............... (*name local school*).

She said, "Too bad, too bad." (*shake head sorrowfully and speak in a high squeaky voice*);

Then she went on her way *(wave good-bye)*.

Soon I heard the roar of a motorcycle *(make sound of engine)*.

It was a tough-looking member of the Hell's Angels *(step forward, give thumbs up)*

He said, "Hey! Need any help?" *(low, grizzly voice while leaning over and looking down)*.

Then he jumped down *(jump up and down once)*,

And tore off his leather jacket *(pretend to take coat off)*,

And wrapped it around me *(move hands in circular wrapping motion)*.

Then he lifted me onto his motorcycle *(mimic lifting and placing body gently)*,

And slowly we went on our way *(hold hands as if gripping handlebars, make roaring sound of engine)*.

Until we came to a Holiday Inn *(make sound of screeching brakes)*.

He carried me inside *(arms outstretched in carrying position)*,

Laid me on a bed *(pretend to place body on bed)*,

And paid the manager a hundred bucks *(mimic handing out the bills)*.

"Take care of my buddy," he said *(rough, tough voice, one hand outstretched, palm up)*,

"I'll take care of the cost" *(both hands now palms up)*.

Then this grizzly looking member of the Hells Angels went on his way *(grab the handlebars and make the sound of the engine again)*.

Now I ask you *(point finger at audience)*,

Which one loved me in the spirit of Jesus *(point to three imaginary people)*:

The minister who said, "Can't stop now, sonny"? *(hold arms akimbo and shake head)*

The schoolteacher who said, "Too bad, too bad"? *(snap fingers once)*

Or the tough looking guy from the Hell's Angels *(hold hands as if gripping handlebars, make sound of engine)*.

Go thou *(point to one side of audience)*,

And do likewise *(sweeping motion to the other side)*.

THE FACE OF JESUS

by Patricia Wells

CHARACTERS

JESUS
BARABBAS

BARABBAS. Welcome to death row.

JESUS. Death row?

BARABBAS. Yeah, there's just four of us here. You don't play poker, do you? We could get up a game.

JESUS. Who are the other two?

BARABBAS. Couple buddies of mine. Got caught stealing. Just thieves. Whadja in for?

JESUS. I'm not sure.

BARABBAS. You mean you're innocent? Welcome to the club.

JESUS. I think it's called Aggravated Conspiracy to Cause Dissension.

BARABBAS. Hey, that's a new one. Who dreamed that up?

JESUS. Our religious leaders.

BARABBAS. No kiddin'! Oh well. Guess what I'm in for?

JESUS. Murder?

BARABBAS. Hah.

JESUS. Sedition?

BARABBAS. What does that mean?

JESUS. It means you tried to overthrow the government. You killed people. You raped. You…

BARABBAS. Okay, okay, whatever. Anyway, my name's Jesus. What's yours?

JESUS. That's my name, too.

BARABBAS. My old man was Abbas. So I'm really Jesus bar Abbas. You can call me Barabbas. Everybody else does.

JESUS. I'm just Jesus. Jesus bar Joseph.

BARABBAS. Your old man was Joseph?

JESUS. In a way.

BARABBAS. Whaddya mean in a way? Was he or wasn't he?

JESUS. It's kind of complicated.

BARABBAS. Yeah, sure. *(pause)* Hey! Why do you keep looking at me like that?

JESUS. Like what?

BARABBAS. You despise me, don't you?

JESUS. Not at all.

BARABBAS. You've got that holier-than-thou look in your eyes. I can tell. Just because I'm a murderer and you didn't kill nobody. You think you're better than me, don't you?

JESUS. Not at all.

BARABBAS. Okay... You feel sorry for me then.

JESUS. Well, yes. I do.

BARABBAS. Well, I don't need your pity! Don't waste your precious pity on me, Jesus bar Joseph. Who are you to pity anybody anyhow? We're both gonna hang, you know! And when they take us down we'll both be dead as doornails.

JESUS. That's why I feel sorry for you.

BARABBAS. Yeah, well, like I say, I don't need your pity. You can feel sorry for yourself.

JESUS. It's not exactly pity.

BARABBAS. What is it then?

JESUS. Try compassion.

BARABBAS. Compassion? What's that?

JESUS. Well, love. You know what love is, don't you?

BARABBAS. Yeah, well my definition of love probably ain't the same as yours buddy.

JESUS. Did you love your mother?

BARABBAS. 'Course I did. *(pause)* But I wasn't the only one.

JESUS. Tell me about her.

BARABBAS. My old lady?

JESUS. Yes.

BARABBAS. Put it this way. I don't know who my father was except he was some guy called Abbas. I only had one father.... But I sure had lots of uncles. If you get my drift.

JESUS. I get your drift.

BARABBAS. What about YOUR old lady?

JESUS. My mother?

BARABBAS. Yeah. What's she like?

JESUS. She's a sweet brave lady who long ago wrapped me in swaddling clothes and laid me in a manger. She's the woman who sits behind a computer all day making data entries. She's the woman who works in a home for people with AIDs and holds their hands when they die. She's the woman in India who sweeps the streets all day with a broom….

BARABBAS. (*interrupting*) Hah. What about the lady who sits on a bar stool with a drink in her hand and says, "Hi ya handsome? New in town?" Is she your mother?

JESUS. Yes.

BARABBAS. Then maybe we're brothers.

JESUS. Maybe we are.

BARABBAS. You really are 'round the bend up the whatji-macallit, aren't you? But, hey, you just may be crazy enough to get us out of here. Let's escape!

JESUS. There is no escape.

BARABBAS. 'Course there is! It's the oldest trick in the book, and we've got a guard dumb enough to fall for it. Look. You pretend to be sick. Just start gagging or croaking or something and I'll call the guard. He comes running, sees you lying on the floor, bends over, I grab him, take the keys, kill him and we're outta here.

JESUS. I told you, Barabbas. There is no escape. For either of us.

BARABBAS. Oh, come on. We're gonna die anyway. What's to lose? We can at least – What's the matter with you!!! Standing there like a helpless idiot. A crazy, stupid, helpless (*pause*) Hey!…Where'd you say you was from?

JESUS. Nazareth.

BARABBAS. Nazareth…a hillbilly from…Hey, wait a minute.

You're Jesus, right? Jesus of Nazareth...Oh my God... You're the guy everybody's talking about. The nutcase that's been going 'round the countryside stirring up all kinds of trouble....Hey guys! My cellmate's a preacher! Whadja think of that? *(to Jesus)* Just don't preach at me, huh?

JESUS. I don't preach at anyone.

BARABBAS. Whadja mean? Whaddaya do then?

JESUS. I tell the truth.

BARABBAS. Oh yeah. Love your neighbour. Love your enemy. I've heard it all.

JESUS. There's one thing more.

BARABBAS. What's that?

JESUS. Love your God.

BARABBAS. God! What's he ever done for me?

JESUS. He just gave you a friend.

BARABBAS. Who?

> (JESUS *smiles.*)
>
> You?
>
> (JESUS *smiles again.*)
>
> You're no friend. You're no...help at all.

JESUS. Wait and see.

BARABBAS. The only thing we've got waiting for us is our last meal. Hey, dija put in your order yet? Whadja gonna get?

JESUS. I'm not hungry.

BARABBAS. Don't be nuts. We can get anything we want. Grab it while you can.

JESUS. I had my last meal last night.

BARABBAS. You did? Whadja have?

JESUS. Bread and wine.

BARABBAS. That all?

JESUS. Those who had it with me will remember.

BARABBAS. Yeah? And who was that?

JESUS. A dozen of my closest friends.

BARABBAS. Some friends. Where are they now?

JESUS. They're waiting.

BARABBAS. Waiting? For what?

JESUS. To see what will happen to me.

BARABBAS. I can tell you what's gonna happen. You're gonna DIE. Same as me. Sunset tomorrow. Poof. We'll be gone. *(scornfully)* "Waiting to see what will happen…" You're not even brave, are you? There're tears in your eyes. I can see 'em from here. All that preacher talk 'bout God and heaven and the silly old angels…You're just as scared as the rest of us.

JESUS. It's true, Barabbas. My eyes ARE filling up. I can tell you I'm not looking forward to what they're going to do to us tomorrow. But I also feel terrible for my people, for Jerusalem, for the whole…

BARABBAS. *(overlapping)* There you go again. Getting all soppy and delusional. I tol'ja. I don't need your pity. What I need is co-operation. Come on! Shake a leg. Let's trick that dumb guard and get outta here. Whaddya say?

JESUS. I think you know what I'm going to say.

BARABBAS. *(losing it)* WHY ARE YOU SO STUBBORN? *(to the guards)* Oops. Sorry. Sorry, governor. I'll keep my voice down. *(to* **JESUS***)* Don't shout, they say, everybody needs their sleep. Great. Few hours from now we're all gonna be six feet under sleeping forever. *(losing it again)* IN THE MEANTIME, WHY DON'T YOU SHUT YOUR OWN … Oops. Sorry. Sorry, again… What? No, no, I wasn't… What?…… WHAAAT???

(long pause)

Okay, let me get this straight. You're saying one of us can walk outta here, free as a bird, no strings attached, just… GO…. Ha. Ha…. I can tell you who that's gonna be. Goody two shoes over there. The little preacher boy who never hurt a flea. WHY ARE YOU TORMENTING

ME LIKE…? Whaaat? Whadja say?... It's *not* him?... It's me?.... I can go free?.... The cell door's wide open. I just walk out and…? No, look. There's gotta be a mistake. I mean…let's face it I'm as guilty as hell 'n everybody knows it. My friend over there, he might be a little funny in the head but he never hurt nobody. We all know that.

JESUS. Whatever happened to the hardened criminal, Barabbas?

BARABBAS. *(ignoring* JESUS, *his attention fixed on the jailer)* What's that? No more gabbing. Just…get the hell out of here?

JESUS. There's no escape, Barabbas. But I'm glad you're free.

BARABBAS. *(laughing)* You're darn right I'm free. I'm outta here, buddy. I'm HISTORY!

*(*BARABBAS *exits.)*

JESUS. Father…I pray for his soul. He needs you. In his crazy, mixed-up, violent way he's crying out for you. Touch his heart and give him peace. *(pause, then calling to the guard)*

All right!…I'm ready.

*(*JESUS *exits down the church aisle. A long pause, then…)*

BARABBAS. *(laughing)* Well, I'm back! Everybody else is gone and I'm still kicking. Howdja like that!

(There's a mood change now as BARABBAS *becomes serious for once.)*

Okay, okay. I know it's not all fun and games. I stayed around, you know, and watched my cell mate go down. It wasn't a pretty sight.

Some of his friends were there. Also some women. I think one of them might have been his mother. They were talking, but I couldn't hear what they were saying. And then, I don't know… I just had this crazy urge to…to go up to the cross and touch his poor, bleeding, godforsaken body…..

Just for a second.

BARABBAS. *(cont.)* He looked at me and… I think he tried to say something but all he could do was kinda nod his head. Then somebody shouted my name and I got outta there fast…

I don't know what to make of it all… And now there are these crazy rumours that he could be alive again. I honestly can't believe it. And yet a really weird thing happened to me just the other night.

I was prowling the streets and I came across a body lying in a gutter. Turned out it was our old guard of all people. He'd been attacked, I guess, and I decided to have the honor of finishing him off.

But just as I raised my dagger, he opened his eyes and groaned and honest to God… I found myself looking into the face of Jesus.

I turned and ran.

I'm still kinda running, still trying to figure it all out.

(pause)

How 'bout you? You anywhere closer to the truth? I hope so… I'd hate to think my buddy died in vain.